# Shamrock Queen

(Always Reddy)

By MARGUERITE HENRY

Illustrated by Wesley Dennis

SCHOLASTIC 

BOOK SERVICES

Published by Scholastic Book Services, a division
of Scholastic Magazines, Inc., New York, N. Y.

To David and Danny Haag

Our appreciation to the Knightscroft Kennels for their cooperation.

M. H. and W. D.

 This Scholastic Book Services edition is published by arrangement with McGraw-Hill Book Co., Inc.

3rd printing . . . . November 1963

Manufactured in the U.S.A.

# CONTENTS

# SHAMROCK QUEEN

Shamrock Queen! That was her official name in the American Field Stud Book. But to Mr. Hoops, her master, she was simply Reddy, the best bird dog up and down the river.

The things that Irish setter could do! She could scent birds even in dry weather when other dogs just sat down on their haunches and gave up. She could find them if they were hidden in a haystack. She could fly over brush and fences and brooks as if she had wings on her feet instead of feathers.

But even more wonderful, Reddy was a dog that knew what to do after she found her birds. She froze into a signpost, pointing to them not only with her nose and her tail, but with every muscle and fiber of her body. And she kept on pointing until her master got there, no matter how long it took.

Even then her work was not done. When Mr. Hoops drove the birds from cover and brought them down with his gun, Reddy retrieved them. Sometimes she had to swim an icy stream to recover them. Sometimes she had to slash her way through briers. But she seemed to thrive on these hardships. At the end of the day she still wore a doggy grin, and her tail was as merry as a flag in the breeze.

Naturally Mr. Hoops loved Reddy. If she so much as sniffed someone else in friendly fashion he felt a twinge of jealousy. As for letting anyone else hunt over Reddy, he stoutly refused.

Mr. Hoops was thinking all these thoughts as he walked home from his office in the Belleville City Hall one late afternoon in October.

Meanwhile, down in the basement of the Hoops' residence, Reddy herself was lying in a box of straw and feeling strangely happy.

She lifted her head and looked around at her newly born puppies. She rose up on one elbow so as not to disturb them. Then she began to wash them for the third time that afternoon. Suddenly she stopped in the middle of a tongue-

stroke. She flicked her ears at the sound of familiar footsteps on the walk outside. Her tail began to quiver. As the steps came nearer, her tail thumped noisily against the side of the box.

At last Mr. Hoops, her master, stood looking down at her. He was not an especially tall man, but from her bed of straw he towered above her.

How strange was his voice today! How soft and low and full of chuckles as he pulled over a coal scuttle, turned it upside down, and sat upon it.

"Reddy," he said, in an awed, hushed tone, "you've never had such fat bold puppies. And five – no, six in all! You're going to be proud of them. They'll be fast-flying hunters with plenty of bird sense."

The puppies made small grunting sounds, but Reddy only half heard them. The other half of her mind was listening to her master.

"I've never told you this, Reddy," he was saying with a faraway look, "but I spent a whole year getting you to trust me. When you were still a pup I took you on walks in the fields. I let you run wild. I let you chase birds and rabbits and butterflies. Even pieces of thistledown. For a whole year we just played and got acquainted."

Reddy reached up over the box and nudged Mr. Hoops with her nose. "Go on! Tell me more!" she seemed to say.

Mr. Hoops laughed. "What a funny pup you were! Everyone said you'd never make a bird dog. 'Too helter-skelter,' they said. 'You're wasting your time, Adam Hoops!' "

Reddy cocked her head and looked enormously interested.

"At night I let you sleep under my bed," Mr. Hoops went on. "And gradually you began training yourself. First you began fetching things. When the alarm clock rang in the

morning, you fetched my socks. Sometimes you even fetched my trousers and suspenders. Remember the time my suspenders caught on a chair leg and snapped in your face? Remember how furious you were?"

Again Reddy nudged Mr. Hoops. "More! More!" she begged with her eyes.

"Then one frosty morning in fall," said Mr. Hoops, as he scratched Reddy's nose, "you pointed a bevy of quail and I said, 'Steady!' This time you did not chase the birds out of the field. You froze into a statue of a dog, and pointed the birds for me as natural-like as if you'd been doing it all your life. And from that moment on, you and I were partners."

Reddy sank back in the straw, enjoying the soft voice of her master and the squirming warmth of her puppies. Usually the master spoke only a single word. "Fetch!" "Heel!" "Stay!" "Steady!" Those were words she understood. But all this stream of talk tumbling from his lips at one time was quite different. Only occasionally her mind pounced upon a familiar word. The rest of the time she did not even try to understand.

Now the master reached in among the puppies and singled out one of them. It was red gold, except for a tiny snippet of white down its nose.

"You and your white snippet," the master crooned, as he let the puppy nuzzle his ear. "*You'll* hunt with spirit. How does the name Snippet appeal to you, little fellow?"

Reddy frowned. Those tones the master was using! They were usually saved for her ears alone. Never before had she heard the master use them to another.

She shook off her puppies. She stepped out of the box in almost human dignity. With a gentle mouth she withdrew Snippet from her master's arms and dropped him alongside the others. Then she laid her own head in the cradle of her master's hand.

"Look here," she seemed to say, as she gazed up at him with reproachful eyes, "we'll take good care of this pup, of course, but he can't come between *partners!*"

Mr. Hoops' eyes twinkled. "Why, Reddy! I believe you are jealous of your own pup," he said. Then he scratched the roots of her ears and ran his finger along the groove between her eyes.

Reddy pushed up closer to enjoy the warmth of his hands. Then, hearing little whining noises from the nest, she got back into her box, taking care not to step on her puppies.

# DOG HAIRS

A tap sounded on the floor above and the master was gone.

In a few minutes two voices came skirling down through the furnace pipes. They were not angry voices at all. Nor were the words spoken quickly. Perhaps it was their very slowness and the way they were said distinctly that made them seem important.

Without knowing why, Reddy felt troubled.

"Have you decided?" came the clear voice of Mrs. Hoops.

"Yes," replied Mr. Hoops, chuckling. "There's a little fellow with a snippet of white between his eyes. From the way he noses his mother I think he'll be a good bird finder."

"He's the one to take Reddy's place?"

It was a long time before Mr. Hoops answered. Then he said soberly, "It's a bit of a shock when you say it out like that, Hannah, but maybe that *was* in the back of my mind."

Then he cleared his throat. "Snippet's still a pup," he said. "Reddy and I will have a long time to train him together."

Downstairs in her box, Reddy found it difficult to breathe. She was panting heavily.

"I've been meaning to tell you, Adam," said the woman's voice.

There was the sound of a coffee cup returned to its saucer, then a pause.

"Tell me what?"

"I've asked Mamma to come and live with us. You know I've been worried about her being alone."

Mr. Hoops laughed out. "Why, that's fine, Hannah. Fine! Now maybe my socks will be darned," he said, jokingly, "and we'll have johnnycake and fried apples for breakfast!"

Reddy's tail began to wag at the gaiety in Mr. Hoops' voice.

"Adam," said Mrs. Hoops, as if it took a great deal of courage to bring out the words. "Mamma cannot live in the same house with dogs."

Mr. Hoops' chair scraped across the floor, and Reddy knew her master was upset. Then Mrs. Hoops' voice went on, hurrying over the words as if they were full of thorns that scratched her throat.

"You see, dear, Mamma is allergic to dog hairs. They make her sneeze and wheeze."

"No!" explained Mr. Hoops. "I've never heard of such a thing."

"Oh, come now, Adam. Cheer up! There really are good dog kennels, you know. And you can visit Reddy every day and hunt over her just as you always did. Besides, Mamma won't be here until the middle of November. That leaves nearly six weeks to sell what pups you can, and to find a nice pleasant kennel for Reddy and the pup that is to take her place."

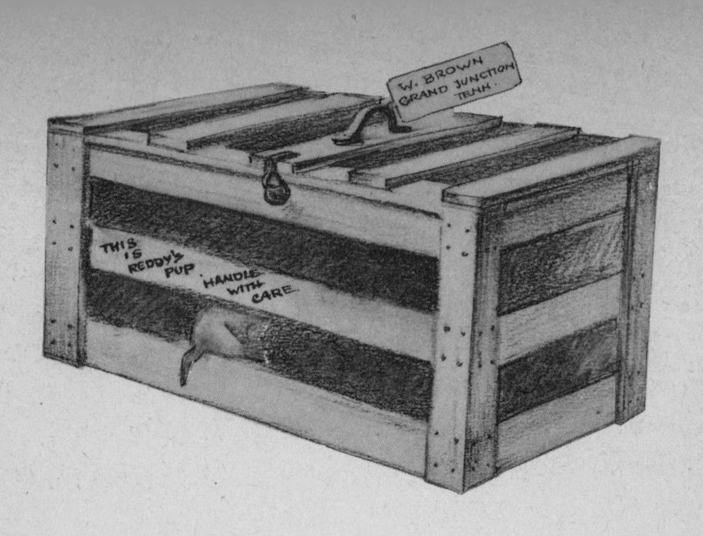


# FIVE PUPS LEAVE HOME

For Reddy the days that followed were completely happy. No more disturbing words came down through the furnace pipes. A sort of peace filled the basement. The morning sunbeams slanting through the small window touched off the six puppies until their coats flamed into red gold.

Other autumns Reddy would have felt a great longing to be outdoors, ranging the fields, testing the wind for the warm scent of birds. But now she was content just to stay in her box, polishing her puppies. Yet in some way she knew that she was pleasing her master as surely as when she pointed a bevy of quail.

It was a busy time for Mr. Hoops. He was City Treasurer for the river town of Belleville, and between his duties at the cream-colored City Hall and watching over the puppies he scarcely had time to think that the hunting season would be over and done with before Reddy could leave her family.

One morning when he noticed that Snippet and two of his litter brothers were getting more milk than they needed while the other pups were pushed aside, Mr. Hoops took matters into his own hands. He dusted off a big picnic hamper and lined it with wool. Then he tucked Snippet and the other greedy ones into the warm folds of wool. Meanwhile the littlest pups nursed until their sides became round as pumpkins. After a while he would release the three from the hamper and the family would be united again.

The picnic hamper seemed made for this procedure. It was nicely ventilated and the lid hooked on securely so that Reddy could not lift her puppies out.

When Mrs. Hoops discovered her favorite picnic hamper serving as a puppy bassinet, she pressed her lips into a firm line. "Adam!" she exclaimed in a voice that boded no good. But she did not go on. She stopped short as if suddenly remembering that soon Reddy would be gone. "Adam," she said to Mr. Hoops' complete surprise, "what a good idea to use the picnic hamper!"

Then their eyes met in a wistful smile of understanding.

At the end of nine days all the puppies began to open their eyes, and Mr. Hoops decided it was high time they learned to lap milk from a dish. He carried pan after pan of warm sweetened milk to the basement. First he dipped his finger into the milk and let the puppies lick it. Then he smeared their muzzles with it, and soon they were licking their jowls to get all the good taste. In less than two weeks they were lapping milk lustily.

Always before, Mr. Hoops had taken his vacation in fall so that he could hunt with Reddy. But this year, instead of hunting prairie chicken in Canada or ruffed grouse in Pennsylvania, he found himself heating milk six times a day. And the thing that amazed him was that he did not mind it at all. A great satisfaction filled him. He found himself singing as he worked, a thing he had not done in years. And one morning he actually caught himself going on about the smartness of his pups to the boys at the City Hall!

Often now, Mr. Hoops slipped away to the telephone booth at the corner drugstore, so that Reddy could not overhear him.

The telephone conversations were pretty much alike.

"That you, Fred?" they would begin. "Reddy's had a fine lot of pups. If you'd like one, they'll be ready for new homes in a few weeks."

Pause.

"Well, if you change your mind, come around the first week in November."

"What's that you say? Gun-shy? Not these Irishmen! Nothing timid about them! Even now they wag their tails at thunder. They'll be rugged game finders. Maybe they'll be field-trial winners. Who knows?"

Pause.

"O.K., Fred, we'll be expecting you."

The first week in November came. One after another Reddy's pups were carried out of the basement in strange arms. Sometimes children carried them out, holding them

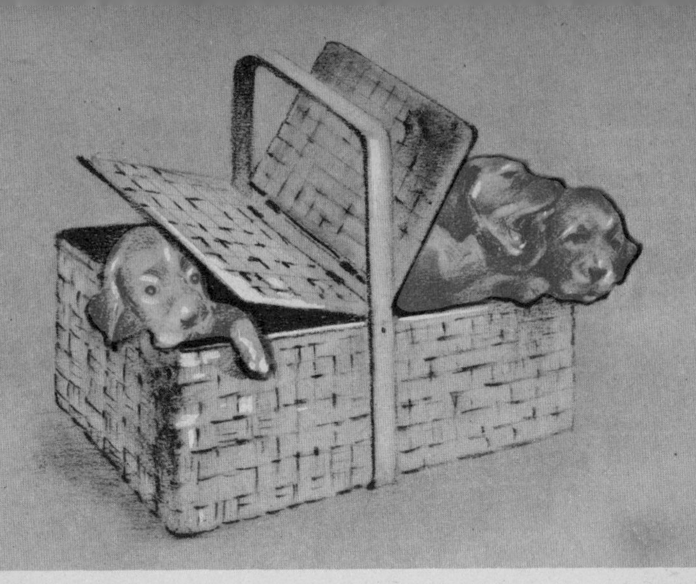

much too tightly. One was crated and shipped to Grand Junction, Tennessee. A spry little grandmother came for another.

The box in the basement looked quite empty when Snippet was the only youngster left. Reddy had a lot of spare time now and she gave all of it to him.

For minutes at a time Mr. Hoops stood looking down at them fondly. He could not bear to think of sending them to a kennel. Reddy was no longer young. This might very well be her last puppy. Before, when he had sold or given her litter away he was comforted with thought that some day she

would have another family. But this time he was not so sure.

Reddy, too, must have felt this, for she refused to let Snippet out of her sight. It was as if her whole life centered in this fat, silken creature. She even tried to play with him, almost knocking him over with her paw and then making it up to him by licking him affectionately with her pink tongue.

# OFF ADVENTURING

It was exactly six weeks to the day when the problem of Reddy and Snippet solved itself.

Mr. and Mrs. Hoops were at the breakfast table. Mrs. Hoops was sugaring her porridge with one hand and holding a color chart in the other.

"Adam," she said, "have you found a place for Reddy and Snippet? Mamma arrives next week, you know. The dogs should be gone now. I've the cleaning to see about, and the decorators will be in tomorrow."

Mr. Hoops did not answer at once. All week he had avoided looking at calendars as if he wore blinders. But now time had caught up with him.

And then a curious thing happened. Mr. Hoops was never able to explain it afterward. He began to talk in a calm voice as if he had carefully thought things out. But he really had not thought them out at all. It was as if someone were whispering in his ear, telling him what to say.

"Why, bless my soul!" he exclaimed, looking innocently enough over the top of his newspaper. "Everything," he went on slowly, "*everything* is taken care of."

"Oh?" said Mrs. Hoops, and the little word ran clear up the scale in surprise.

"Yes," he repeated calmly, and to his own amazement. "Mayor Twitterton and the Commissioners down at the City Hall are going to have both Reddy and her pup."

Mrs. Hoops' mouth fell open, but not to take the spoonful of porridge which she held in mid-air. "Both Reddy *and* her pup?" she questioned.

"Both Reddy and her pup," he repeated, feeling terribly proud of the Mayor and his co-workers.

"They want them both?" she asked, unbelieving.

Mr. Hoops nodded. It was as simple as that.

Without waiting to finish her breakfast, Mrs. Hoops jumped up from the table. She began gathering together all of Reddy's belongings. There was her leash and the ball with the tinkling bell inside it. There was her old rubber bone and her earthenware drinking bowl. Mrs. Hoops was rather a large woman and usually she moved slowly and majestically. But this morning she fairly danced around the kitchen.

"How much better this is than having Reddy and Snippet boxed up in a kennel!" she sang out gaily. "You know, Adam, I've misjudged Mr. Twitterton. I knew he was the best Mayor Belleville ever had, but somehow I thought he would be too neat and orderly to put up with dog hairs."

Mr. Hoops was swallowing a last sip of coffee. He choked and felt as if he were drowning in his own cup. All his calm

assurance was gone. He sat there tongue-tied, trying to think how the Mayor really did feel about dogs.

He watched the growing pile of things at the door. He remembered wistfully when he had hung the rubber bone in its cellophane wrapper on the topmost bough of the Christmas tree, and Reddy had noticed it first thing. She had stood up on her hind feet and snuffed it out from all the tinsel and baubles.

The City Hall clock was striking eight. It put an end to Mr. Hoops' memories. He crumpled his paper napkin and stuffed it in his empty water glass. With an uneasy feeling in the pit of his stomach, he got up, hastily wrapped Reddy's bowl and her toys in the morning newspaper, and folded his topcoat over the queer looking package. Then he put on his hat which hung on a peg in the kitchen and tiptoed down the basement stairway.

Reddy and Snippet were at the foot of the stairs, wild with excitement. Reddy had heard the faint tinkle of her bell, and the click of her leash against the eathenware bowl. She made a flying leap to lick Mr. Hoops' face, then raced in wide circles around and around, stopping only to nip her puppy's ear or to roll over and over in joy.

Mr. Hoops' worry lines disappeared. "We're off!" he cried. "We're off! Adventuring! This, my friends, is a turning point!"

He lifted Snippet and set him in the crook of his arm. "I'll carry your youngster upstairs, Reddy," he said, "but from then on you do the carrying."

And Reddy did. At street crossings she picked Snippet up in her mouth, threaded her way through the small-town traffic, and then dropped him safely on the other side.

Children on their way to school squealed with delight at sight of Reddy carrying her puppy. Grown-ups, too, stopped to pat Snippet and to say they had missed seeing Reddy. In a small town like Belleville, it was important news when a dog like Shamrock Queen had pups.

As for Reddy, she was dizzy with happiness. Holding her head high and her tail on an even level with her back, she moved along with an airy grace. Now and again as they passed some homey cottage there was the delicious smell of sausages or bacon and eggs frying. But even more enticing were the winds that blew from the fields beyond the cottages. Reddy's nose twitched. Faintly but unmistakably she caught the scent of birds.

Suddenly she stopped, frozen in her tracks. Nose in the air, tail well up, left forepaw raised slightly, she was stretched out in a beautiful point.

Mr. Hoops coughed. To his great embarrassment Reddy was pointing at a parked car in which two men were poring over a road map. "Reddy," he said under his breath, "there are no birds here. Come away. Come away, I tell you!"

But Reddy continued to point while Snippet was trying his best to copy her.

Just then the driver of the car glanced up. "Look, Fergy!" he roared as he nudged his companion. And then he threw back his head and laughed until the car windows rattled. His friend looked up, puzzled. Then he, too, caught sight of Reddy and broke into laughter. He reached into the back of the car, and held up three ringneck pheasants for Mr. Hoops to see.

"That dog has a nose, sir," he called out. "Wouldn't want to sell her or her pup, would you? I'm needing a smart hunter. Pay you a good price, too."

Mr. Hoops shook his head in great pride. "Not for sale at any price," he replied. "Come, Reddy. It's nearly eight-thirty. We must step along."

Reddy leaped into great long strides. She turned around now to see how her youngster was keeping up. What a clown he was! Waddling along with short hurried steps, trying to snap at the dry leaves whirling about his feet, trying to keep up with his big mother.

Just before they reached the City Hall, Mr. Hoops snapped Reddy's leash to her collar.

"We'll not look any farther ahead than the white snippet on Snippet's nose," he said soothingly. "Let come what may."

# A GOOD MOVE!

With his thumb on the latch of the City Hall door, Mr. Hoops paused. Then he squared his shoulders, took a deep breath, and walked in as if there were nothing unusual in coming to work with a mother dog and her pup.

What a commotion they caused! Bessie, the Mayor's elderly stenographer, came shrieking out of her office at sight of Reddy and Snippet. One after another, the four Commissioners came running out of their offices. Even Mayor Twitterton wanted to know what the noise was about. Two citizens of Belleville who had just stopped in to pay their

taxes joined the circle which was now completely closed in by Katy, the scrubwoman.

Reddy felt as if she could hardly breathe. How stifling the air seemed! There were so many strange scents – the Mayor's bay rum, Katy's brown-soapy smell, and the choking odor from the gilt on the radiators.

Everyone began gabbling at once, but Katy's voice climbed the highest. "Lord love the Irish!" she sang out as she stroked Reddy with moist pink hands all crinkled from hot water. "And look at the *little* Irishman, will you!" Then, turning to the Mayor, she said something that gave Mr. Hoops a start.

"You've been wanting to go hunting for years, your Honor," she said. "Sure, and here's Ireland's proudest dogs just waiting to take you."

To his surprise, Mr. Hoops found himself nodding in agreement. If the Mayor would let Reddy and Snippet stay at the City Hall, the least he could do was to let him hunt over Reddy.

Mayor Twitterton smiled. He stooped down and picked up Snippet right from Reddy's nose. But Reddy, for some reason known only to herself, did not curl her lips nor snarl. She just watched Snippet closely, ready to spring to his defense at a moment's notice.

"What brings this on, Adam?" asked the Mayor good-naturedly. "Been thrown out of your house?"

Mr. Hoops' face went red. "Not at all, sir. It's just that — it's just that the decorators are coming."

By this time Mr. Hoops' arm was nearly paralyzed from trying to hold all of Reddy's belongings under his topcoat.

"I'll just settle these two in the basement," he said.

The Mayor set Snippet down on the floor. In one leap Reddy reclaimed him and began licking his coat frantically. Then she picked him up in her mouth and followed Mr. Hoops down the winding stairway. At the foot of the stairs she dropped him quickly.

In a flash, the two dogs were everywhere at once, exploring the room where supplies were kept, the coal room, the furnace room.

Reddy's nose told her that a mouse was building a fluffy nest inside an old umbrella; that a cat who dined on fish and cream lived in the coal bin. She sniffed noisily, surveying the basement in her dog's way.

At last she came back to Mr. Hoops and raised a pair of lively eyes to his.

"A good move!" she said, as plainly as if she could talk.

Then she and Snippet sat down in a little patch of sunlight and watched while Mr. Hoops lined a big box with packing straw, placed it close to the warmth of the furnace, and filled the earthenware crock with fresh cold water.

Reddy jumped into the box. She pawed the straw vigorously to shape it into a nest. Then she reached overboard and grabbed Snippet, who was squealing and trying to climb up the slippery sides.

Snippet did not waste a minute. He nuzzled up to his mother as if to say, "This, now — *this* is snug."

Mr. Hoops smiled in satisfaction. Then with a comforting word and a pat on each glossy head he went upstairs to his desk, adjusted his green eyeshade and fastened celluloid guards around his shirt sleeves.

"Tsk! Tsk!" he said under his breath as he noted that the clock on the wall said nine-thirty. And "tsk! tsk!" he said again as he saw that it hung crooked. Being an orderly soul, he tried to straighten it, but when a tiny chip of plaster fell to the floor, he decided to leave well enough alone.

"Remind janitor to get longer screw for clock," he wrote on his desk pad. Then, humming a bar or two from *"When Irish Eyes Are Smiling,"* he settled down to the business of the morning with a light heart.

Down in the basement Reddy nosed Snippet from head to tail. She gave him an extra good licking to clean off the faintest scent of bay rum. Then she laid her big fringy paw over his shoulder.

Now she began to doze off. Dimly, she could hear her master clear his throat, and occasionally she heard the measured tread of his footsteps.

A deep peace filled the box and made itself heard in Snippet's soft puppy sighs and Reddy's snoring.

# DOG MULLIGAN

Things could not have worked out better if Mr. Hoops *had* planned them.

When Katy mentioned hunting to Mayor Twitterton, she brought back an old dream to his mind. The dream grew until the Mayor had visions of himself bringing down pheasant and quail and woodcock in great numbers.

He began to think of Reddy and Snippet as *his* brace of gun dogs and of Mr. Hoops as their handler. He encouraged Mr. Hoops to begin training Snippet at the earliest possible moment. "And if that requires a little time off from your duties as City Treasurer," he said with a chuckle, "that is quite all right, Adam."

Meanwhile the two dogs were treated as honored guests. Mornings were filled with endless surprises. The Mayor and the four Commissioners and Katy all came to work hiding little brown paper sacks in their brief cases or inside their purses or pockets.

Then, one at a time, they tiptoed down the stairs when no one else was looking and opened their sacks.

"See!" the Mayor would whisper while the scent of his bay rum floated through the basement. "I've brought you some nice chicken bones. But," he added, "you two can earn them all right! When the hunting season rolls around I'll expect you to find me the plumpest birds that ever went into a pie." And he patted his stomach and shut his eyes in pleasant anticipation.

Apparently the mayor did not know the danger of giving chicken bones to dogs. But, as luck would have it, the bones were picked so clean that neither dog was the least bit interested in them. As soon as the Mayor had gone back upstairs Reddy would carry the bones to Victoria, the black cat that lived in the coal bin. Victoria would open a sleepy eye, stretch, and throw a scornful glance at the bones as if to say, "Just drop them anywhere. You seem to forget that I'm used to salmon and cream! I have friends upstairs too, you know."

And she really had. Bessie, the stenographer, fed her so well that she completely ignored the mice in the basement.

The bones that Katy offered, however, were not at all like the Mayor's. They were big and knuckly and wonderfully sweet to gnaw upon. Reddy and Snippet liked Katy.

"Look, my fine Irishmen," she would murmur softly. "Katy's got a surprise for the two of you. 'Tis an elegant knuckle bone for Reddy and a wee little nubbin for Snippet. Something to keep your teeth strong and your minds busy all the long day."

And so the days went by, happily enough. For Reddy, however, nighttimes were the best-of-all-times. Then her master spent two full hours with her. It never occurred to her that he came to see Snippet, too, and she was completely happy in not knowing.

After a rough-and-tumble greeting, Mr. Hoops would set about to prepare "dog mulligan" on a little gas plate in the basement. Dog mulligan was a dish to make Reddy and Snippet drool. First Mr. Hoops cut up generous chunks of meat. Then he cooked them slowly in a pot with vegetables. Sometimes it was beef stewed with celery and great slices of Spanish onion. Sometimes it was lamb cut up with carrots and peas. And sometimes it was thick slices of liver with tomatoes.

While the mulligan simmered, the master took Reddy and Snippet on long walks. If there was a full moon, they went far beyond the village, far beyond city smells.

The dogs sucked the clean air into their lungs. They went crazy with the smell of it. They tested it for bird scent. Often Reddy pointed quail, only to have Snippet rush past her and flush the birds into the air.

"We'll teach that rascal of yours not to flush your birds, won't we, Reddy?" the master would say. And though the talk between Mr. Hoops and Reddy was one-sided, it was always as partner to partner.

With appetites sharpened by exercise, the dogs returned to the City Hall, where the meat and vegtables, stewing in their own juices, sent forth rich fragrance.

Red tongues licked with eagerness as Mr. Hoops dished up the mulligan and crumbled dry toast into each steaming bowl. "It's the little crunchy pieces of toast," he would say, "that make the brown gravy taste the sweeter." And then he stirred and stirred, his spoon making music against the sides of the bowl.

The dogs drolled uncontrollably, and no one scolded at the little drops of water that fell from their jaws to the floor.

"Speak!" commanded the master when the stirring was done and the mulligan had cooled off.

Reddy let out a ringing bark of joy, and in a matter of weeks Snippet could add his own puppy voice to his mother's.

Instead of watching the two dogs eat, the master went upstairs so they could gulp their food in peace and privacy. He used these few moments to try the safe and see that his cage-like office was in order. Then he called Reddy and Snippet for a final turn about the village green before bedtime.

Secretly, Mr. Hoops enjoyed this little stroll as much as the dogs did. As a boy he had wanted to be a policeman, and now on these walks he liked to watch Policeman O'Toole as he controlled the one and only traffic light in Belleville. Simply by turning a hande, Policeman O'Toole could switch the light from red to green and back again.

"Top of the evening to you!" Officer O'Toole always said. "And for two of my own countrymen," he added with a nod toward Reddy and Snippet, "traffic can wait. Green she goes!"

Then, with a flick of his wrist accompanied by a small clicking sound, the light went as green as the Emerald Isle.

If Reddy and Snippet had understood Policeman O'Toole's remarks, they could not have shown their appreciation more plainly. They trotted across the street, their tails waving a polite thank-you.

All too soon the walk was over and the dogs were back in the basement where the faint scent of meat and vegetables still lingered. Contented, they settled down to sleep and to wait for morning and their master.

So the winter passed.

# A BRACE OF GUN DOGS

As the days lengthened into spring, it meant but one thing to Mayor Twitterton and to Mr. Hoops: extra hours for training Snippet.

"I'm getting sort of paunchy," the Mayor admitted to Mr. Hoops one day, as he patted his vest. "Shooting over your dogs will not only be good sport, it may thin me down," he laughed. Then his face sobered. "I want you to be the first to know, Adam. I plan to run for Congress."

"No!" exclaimed Mr. Hoops.

"Yes!" nodded the mayor with a boyish smile. "And I think it's time I had a hobby. I've sent away to New York for one of those Super Slim hunting coats lined with moleskin. You want to know something, Adam?"

"What?" asked Mr. Hoops.

The Mayor lowered his voice. "I've always hankered to hunt with a pair of stylish gun dogs. Is Snippet gun-broke yet?"

But Reddy and Mr. Hoops were not "breaking" Snippet. They were playing a game. They were taking him out into the fields and letting him chase anything with wings. Even airplanes!

The day that Snippet thought he had chased a plane out of the field, Reddy cast a quick glance at her master as much as to say, "A rattle-brained scamp, isn't he?" And her teeth showed in a wide grin.

So, in the training of Snippet, the understanding between Reddy and Mr. Hoops grew and strengthened.

Snippet chased rabbits as well as airplanes, but Mr. Hoops soon put an end to that. He built a rabbit hutch behind the City Hall. There, on pleasant Sundays, Snippet was penned in with four pink-eyed rabbits. Of course, Mr. Hoops took the precaution of cutting little rabbit-size exits in the corners of the hutch so the rabbits could escape into an outer pen if Snippet played too rough.

But to Mr. Hoops' amazement, Snippet did not chase the rabbits at all. He only eyed them curiously. Four tame rabbits nibbling away at carrots were no fun at all. Snippet was a sportsman; he preferred his game wild. He just sat in a corner of the pen and howled for freedom.

After several Sundays spent with the rabbits he lost all interest in them, wild *or* tame. "They all smell pretty much alike," he seemed to conclude. And from then on a rabbit could brush him with his powder-puff tail before he would so much as take notice.

The only real training tools Mr. Hoops possessed were his whistle and an old battered hat. Snippet respected both. By the time summer came, he understood as many signals as most dogs twice his age. He knew that one short blast meant "Stop!" If it was followed by a second short blast he knew it meant, "Look to the master for directions." Then, at a mere wave of the hat to the right or to the left, Snippet would range in the direction indicated. But of all signals, Snippet preferred the long blast that meant, "Come in! There may be a choice morsel of food as a reward!"

Snippet's family manners were exceptional, too. He stayed

in the basement where he belonged and never so much as showed his nose upstairs unless he was called. He could walk at heel. He could fetch. He could sit or lie down at a single command. And all of this he had learned as naturally as a nestling learns to fly.

"Perhaps," said Mr. Hoops to Reddy one morning in August, "perhaps that Snippet of yours will show some bird sense today. Let's work him along the riverbank."

The morning air was moist. Even the undersides of the leaves were beaded with dew. It was the kind of day when the brush holds scent particles a long time.

"Come to think of it," mused Mr. Hoops, "it was on such a day as this that you, Reddy, graduated from a harum-scarum pup into a full-fledged bird dog."

With hope running high, Mr. Hoops drove his dogs to the riverbank and turned them loose. At the signal to go, they broke away with a wild dash. It was as if they had been imprisoned for days and now must taste their freedom in a single burst of speed. Reddy shot into the lead with Snippet close on her heels. She was heading for a clump of low-hanging willows.

At the same instant both dogs caught the scent of quail. Reddy snapped into a beautiful point.

Instinctively Snippet pointed too and just as he was about to give chase to the birds, Mr. Hoops blew a single short blast on his whistle.

If Snippet had been a child he might have turned red in the face and screamed, "I won't stop! These birds are mine to chase. Mine! Mine! I found them myself!" But being a dog he bent his will to his master's. For the first time he stood motionless, holding the birds until Mr. Hoops flushed them.

How Mr. Hoops praised the youngster! Even Reddy came over and licked his muzzle.

Snippet thrived on praise. By noon Mr. Hoops scarcely found it necessary to use his whistle, for Snippet was developing good bird sense, and Mr. Hoops believed in letting a dog hunt in his own way.

Snippet proved the wisdom of his method in a way that Mr. Hoops himself never forgot. After a light lunch and a good rest, Mr. Hoops again put the dogs to work. A wind had come up meanwhile and it was laden with bird scent. At the word "Go!" Reddy streaked toward a likely strip of cover. She was nothing but a needle of red whipping in and out among the dark green of the hedgerows. Snippet, however, had ideas of his own. He took several wide swings but finally ranged off in the direction of his mother.

Mr. Hoops reached the brush just in time to see Reddy lock into a perfect point. And then he watched breathlessly as Snippet came up. He saw Snippet look at Reddy. Then, instead of running past her and stealing her point, he did something that to Mr. Hoops was reward enough for all the pans of milk carried into the basement, for all the anxious moments that puppies give their masters.

With his tail at a jaunty angle Snippet stopped dead in his tracks and honored his mother's point. It was a sight Mr. Hoops never forgot. Two golden red dogs standing motionless, pointing the birds that were rightfully theirs. *Now* Mr. Hoops knew he had a brace of gun dogs!

"I feel almost foolish," he admitted to Reddy, "to reward Snippet with a piece of dog-candy when what he really deserves is a diploma with satin ribbons and a gold seal."

Snippet, however, did not feel that way about it at all. He ate the dog-candy with great relish.

The Mayor's face took on a pleased look when, the next day, Mr. Hoops reported that Snippet had passed his training period. They were both in Mr. Hoops' cage-like office. It was almost time for the noon whistle, so the Mayor reached over in front of Mr. Hoops and closed the little window through which Mr. Hoops took in taxes and paid out salaries to the city employees. He even pulled down the shade so no one could peep in. Then he sat down on a stool facing Mr. Hoops.

"Adam," he announced nervously, "I have a letter from the School Board."

For a long moment he said no more. Instead he got down from the stool and walked over to the window, his back toward Mr. Hoops.

It was seldom that Mayor Twitterton was at a loss for words while Mr. Hoops nearly always found conversation difficult. So now Mr. Hoops thought of an encouraging question to help the Mayor along.

"What," he said, "did the School Board have to say?"

The Mayor turned away from the window. "They want me to make a speech," he blurted out quickly. "A speech dedicating the new gymnasium. And it so happens, Adam, that the dedication ceremonies come on the opening day of the shooting season."

"Too bad to miss the first day," Mr. Hoops said, "but . . ."

"That is the very day," the Mayor interrupted, "that the 'Photo News Magazine' is sending a representative by the name of Duke Hall to hunt with me. He's coming all the way from Chicago and he can only stay for the day."

Mr. Hoops' collar suddenly seemed too tight for him. He thought he knew what the Mayor wanted.

"I know how you hate to make speeches, Adam, but I'm asking you to take my place at school. I'll have Bessie make a neat typewritten copy of my address for you. Besides, the ceremonies will be over before noon and you can hop in your car and join us. What do you say?"

# STEADY!

The opening day of the hunting season broke clear and cool with a light wind blowing.

"A perfect day!" sighed Mr. Hoops as he tucked the Mayor's speech in his inside coat pocket. Then, with never a backward glance toward Reddy and Snippet, who were straining out of the Mayor's car windows, he set off hastily in the direction of the school.

"We'll save the plumpest birds for you, Adam," the Mayor called out as he started the car.

The Mayor looked like a plump-chested bird himself in his Super Slim hunting coat which did not live up to its name. Duke Hall, from the "Photo News Magazine," climbed in beside him. Although he was quite young, the photographer's face was the color of weathered oak leaves. And his mouth was broad and ready for laughter.

Now if the Mayor had come right out and said, "Young fellow, this is my first time hunting with a brace of gun dogs," Duke Hall would probably have been quick to understand. As it was, he sat with an amused grin on his face, watching the Mayor, who was now turning down a country lane with but one hand on the heel. With the other, he clutched the whistle that hung around his neck as if it were the mystic signal for filling his gamebag.

"One toot," he mumbled to himself, "means 'Whoa!'

"Two quick toots mean 'Give instructions.'

"A single long blast means 'Come in!' "

Reddy and Snippet hung far out of the windows to escape the smell of the mayor's bay rum.

As the car approached one of Mr. Hoops' favorite hunting spots, Reddy's nose began to quiver in recognition. She caught the scent of a creek and the dense cover that lined its banks, and her tail began to wave in a great arc of happiness. Snippet, too, was sniffing the wind and barking. Both dogs could hardly wait for the mayor to bring the car to a stop, but he scarcely heard their eager yelps.

Still memorizing his signals, he drove on and at last stopped his car before a field of shocked corn. Then he and Duke Hall got out and turned the dogs loose.

"Go!" commanded Mr. Twitterton.

Reddy and Snippet cut across the cornfield, making straight for an old rail fence half hidden by broom grass and ragweed. Memory told them that here was a strip of cover worth looking into. Barely half way to their goal, they heard a sharp blast on the Mayor's whistle.

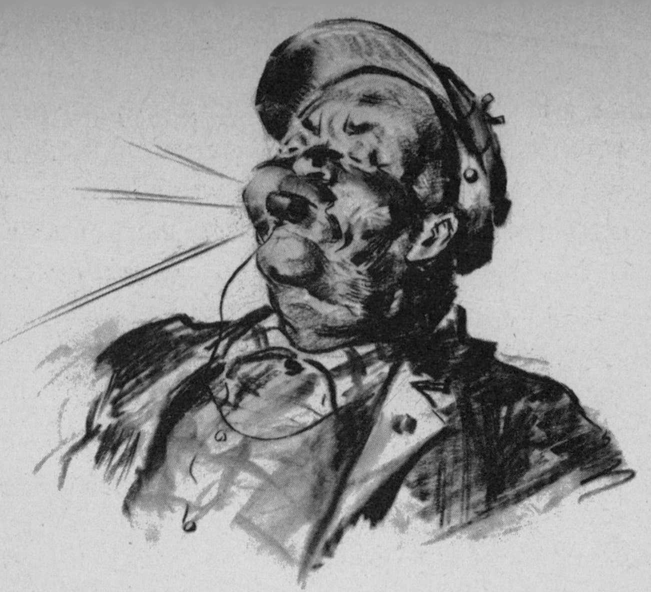

Both dogs halted in their tracks. They were bewildered. This was no time to stop, with the faint scent of birds pulling them on.

Again the whistle shattered the quiet. It was followed by a second short blast. "Stop for directions!" the whistle screamed. Reddy and Snippet looked back, their brows wrinkled.

The Mayor was running to keep up. He was waving his arm wildly to the right, directing the dogs away from the fence.

Obediently they turned and recrossed the cornfield. With a fresh burst of speed they made for the creek which they had passed in the car. Nothing slowed them. They sailed over a fence as easily as if it had been a foot scraper. They leaped over a ditch. They slashed their way through brush and weeds and vines.

"Wrr-r-r-e-e-e-e!" shrilled the whistle, just at the precise moment when both dogs knew that game was near.

The dogs hesitated, their noses in the wind. Then obedience won out, and they tracked back, heads and tails drooping. It was hard to believe that these slow-going creatures were the same pair that had started off so merrily.

Their disgust deepened when the Mayor offered no tasty titbit as a reward for coming in. Instead, he snapped on their leashes. Then the two men and the dogs retraced their way to the car. Duke Hall had forgotten to take his camera out of the car! But what the Mayor did not know was this: he had forgotten it on purpose.

By now the sun was high overhead. The dogs were sulking. They had come to work the fields, not to dance to signals like dogs in a circus.

"Now, Hall," the Mayor winked as he handled the newsman his camera, "we'll get some good shots. And Reddy and Snippet, I've a sharp eye for birds. You just listen to my whistle. All right now," he puffed, as he led the way into a recently burned-over field. "If there are no birds in the cornfield, we'll just cross the road and fill our gamebags." And he released the dogs.

By this time Reddy was so confused that she decided to hunt in her own way. Besides, her nose told her that a burned-over area does not hold scent. To the Mayor's amazement, she wheeled about, cut back across the road and lined out in the direction of her first hunch: the old rail fence, half hidden by broom grass and ragweed. Snippet followed at a merry clip. It looked like a well-laid plan. There was no hesitation on the part of either dog. With an air of decision they were off.

The Mayor was not used to disobedience. He wanted to keep the dogs in close to him. He wanted them to swing back and forth like the pendulum of a clock. He began blowing wildly on his whistle. A single sharp blast. Then a second sharp blast.

This time neither dog heard. They seemed unable to stop. It was as if some inner signal were driving them on, faster and faster. Their ears were whipped back by the wind and the very sweep of their tails said, "Nothing can stop us; we've work to do!"

They were out of sight of the Mayor now. They were reaching out for the scent of quail. They had it. It came to them borne on the wind that passed over the tall weeds. They had found the hiding place of a bevy of quail.

Both Reddy and Snippet located the birds at the same time. In mid-stride they each snapped into a magnificent point.

Long years of training had taught Reddy to hold her point until her master came. No matter how long it took, she must hold the birds for him.

Seconds and minutes wore on. Reddy's left forepaw began to twitch. The shrill whistling had stopped. In its place came the raucous sound of the Mayor's automobile horn.

Reddy continued to stand motionless, except for that slight twitching of her raised paw. But in her mind there was no wavering. Her instinct told her that her master would come. She must remain steady. Steady. He would come.

She forgot about Snippet. She forgot about the Mayor. She only knew that she must be staunch. He would come.

Dimly she heard the scurry of wood folk. Squirrels rummaging among dry leaves. Beavers building their houses. Yet she was scarcely conscious of these little goings on.

Her ears were tuned to only one sound, the familiar footsteps of her master. At last the sound came. Her heart beat faster. She recognized the pattern of those steps. They were coming closer. They were running.

She stiffened her point, holding her nose and tail well up, every muscle in her body tense.

Her master was behind her. He had come! He was moving up, driving the birds from cover. He was shooting over her. And at long last he was saying the welcome words: "Go fetch!"

Reddy's weariness vanished. Eagerly she went out and brought the birds in.

With the game at his feet, Mr. Hoops did not go back to the Mayor at once. He sat down and gathered the big long-legged dog in his arms.

"My old girl," he said softly. "My partner. We trained your youngster well. He finally obeyed the whistle and went back to the Mayor. But you, Reddy, you held your birds." And he took her quivering forepaw in his hand and rubbed it.

# LAZY GIRL

When Mayor Twitterton opened the "Photo News Magazine" the color left his face as he read:

CANDIDATE FOR CONGRESS TRIES TO POINT BIRDS
DOGS OBJECT!

A dozen comical pictures stared back at him. Duke Hall had snapped him blasting away on the whistle, his face puffed into a balloon. He had caught him with his trousers snagged on a barbed-wire fence while the dogs stood by, grinning. In another picture, he was trying to recover his cap from an overhanging branch while the sky was dotted with quail.

"That settles it!" stormed the Mayor. "I'll cancel my subscription to 'Photo News.' What's more, there'll be no more chicken bones for either dog. Ungrateful pups!"

But of course neither Reddy nor Snippet missed the bones. It just saved them the bother of carrying them to Victoria.

Besides, something far more serious was happening to Reddy. It seemed every now and then as if her legs were not her own. They refused to obey her will.

Mornings when she wanted to dance on her hind feet and plant her forepaws on Mr. Hoops' shoulders, she could not make it.

It was worse on a morning after a hard workout in the field, especially if the weather had been frosty and the birds had fallen in water. One morning she felt so stiff and sore that she could not get up until the sun found her bed and toasted her bones. Then, gradually, she limbered up and by noon she seemed as good as ever.

It was strange that Mr. Hoops suspected nothing. If Reddy failed to race and tear about the basement when he arrived, he laid it to sleepiness.

"Why, you lazy old girl!" he would say. "Pretty soft to lie abed all hours.

Then Reddy would make a great effort to rise.

"I declare!" Mr. Hoops would laugh. "You're as stilty-legged as a colt."

On dry sunny days, however, Reddy seemed livelier than ever before. She could put her paws clear up on Mr. Hoops' shoulders with no trouble at all. And she was so glad about it that she gave his ears and neck an extra good licking.

All through the hunting season Snippet gained in skill while Reddy seemed to let down, but Mr. Hoops admitted this to no one. He scarcely admitted it to himself. What if

Reddy did not range out as wide as Snippet? What if she seemed to avoid fences and hedgerows? She still had a sure nose for birds and pointed them like an arrow.

One day several birds that Mr. Hoops hit fell into a creek swollen by fall rains. He watched amazed as Reddy just stood on the bank and let Snippet retrieve them. She made no move to help him.

Mr. Hoops had to call her name out sharply before she finally splashed her way into the water and did her share of the work. Even then Mr. Hoops did not suspect.

It was the last day of the hunting season before Mr. Hoops knew.

The weather was unpromising. In spite of a crust of snow on the ground, the air was dry with a wind so fierce that it scattered all bird scent. As Snippet dashed over the rough country, Reddy seemed almost to crouch along. Mr. Hoops wondered if rheumatism had at last caught up with her, but he closed the little shutters of his mind.

"She's just smart," he told himself. "Saving her strength for a real burst of speed when she needs it."

The day wore itself out. By twilight Mr. Hoops' game-bag was still empty. "I know we should be getting home," he told Reddy and Snippet, "but I always like to take at least one bird to Mrs. Hoops. What do you say to working

the alder thicket once more? The wind seems to be dying a little. Our luck is bound to change."

Snippet wagged his tail in agreement and Reddy seemed more eager than when they had started out. It was almost as if she knew that this was the last hour of the hunting season.

At a wave of the hat both dogs made a beeline for the alder thicket. Now Snippet was clearing a split rail fence. But Reddy! She was not going to clear it. Mr. Hoops watched horrified as she hit the top rail, was catapulted into the air, and then fell in a little heap in the leaves.

It was only a matter of seconds until he reached the spot where she lay, but to him it seemed hours. Snippet had already found her, and when Mr. Hoops reached them he was licking a tiny trickle of blood on her forehead.

He dropped to his knees beside Reddy and pillowed her head in his lap. "She tried to tell me in the only way she knew. Please, God," he prayed, "don't let her die."

He glanced about helplessly. The ground was hummocky, but between the hummocks were pockets of snow. With quick hands he filled his handkerchief with the snow and placed it on Reddy's head. She made no move then nor when he felt of her legs to see if they were broken. He listened to her breathing but could hardly hear it for his own.

"Reddy," he pleaded. "If you'll get well, we'll have the best of days together. I'll rub your legs with warm liniment night and morning. You'll never have to work the fields again. And when spring comes you can lie on a warm rug in the sun and watch me plant my garden. Why, you can sleep all day if you like!"

He took off his jacket and wrapped it closely about her. How quiet the world seemed! A squirrel came to look at them with an inquiring glance, but did not even scold.

Night was closing in when Mr. Hoops felt a stirring in his arms. He pressed his ear against Reddy's muzzle to hear any faint cries of pain. There were none. Reddy was opening her eyes. She was trying to lick Mr. Hoops' face. She was trying to comfort *him!*

Joyously Mr. Hoops carried his precious burden to the car. Then he sped for the warmth of the City Hall.

"Reddy's had an accident," he told Mrs. Hoops over the telephone. "I'll spend the night here. Yes, Hannah, there's a cot to sleep on. I'll be all right."

# THE TIME HAS COME

It was long past midnight before Mr. Hoops slept. He sponged the blood from Reddy's head and cut away some of her matted hair. He bathed the wound with flowers of sulphur. Then he wrapped her in his old hunting coat and placed her near the furnace. She fell into a fitful sleep while he and Snippet looked on.

Mr. Hoops could not help noticing how Snippet had changed. In just a few hours he had grown from a playful youngster into a responsible dog. It was as if he were the parent now and Reddy the overgrown pup to be watched.

"Snippet," said Mr. Hoops softly, "it's time you had your supper. Nothing fancy tonight. Just dry crumbles moistened with beef tea."

While Snippet cleaned his bowl, Mr. Hoops heated some milk, beat an egg into it, and added a little beef tea. Then, very gently, he lifted Reddy's jowl and poured a teaspoonful of the warm liquid between her teeth. She swallowed it and then ever so faintly began to whimper. She could stand the scratch of briers and the thwack of a fence rail, but when the master bent low over her in sympathy she cried.

Now Mr. Hoops moistened his finger in the liquid and let Reddy lick it as if she were a puppy. And soon she was lapping the milk not because she wanted it, but because it seemed to please him.

When she could drink no more, Mr. Hoops examined her carefully. Besides the gash on her head, the pads of her feet were cut by splinters and thorns.

She seemed very tired now, so Mr. Hoops covered her and let her sleep.

Meanwhile he made a table out of a barrel and spread open his dog emergency kit. With skilled fingers he cut and sewed four boots out of white leather. He made them long enough to fit well above Reddy's knees. Then he lined the insides of them with a layer of balsam salve and set them on top of the furnace to warm.

At midnight Reddy woke with a whining cry. She was ashamed of it immediately afterward, for she licked Mr. Hoops' hands as he took out the splinters and the thorns from the feathering between her toes. At last he fitted her paws into the boots he had made and covered her again with his coat. In a very few minutes she began to snore.

With a deep sigh, Mr. Hoops tiptoed upstairs to finish the night on the Mayor's cot.

Reddy's wounds healed like magic. Even her morning lameness improved now that she spent most of her time indoors where it was warm and dry. She could climb stairs as well as ever, and she could dance on her hind feet when she wanted to. In spite of this, she was not happy.

All her life she had been a worker. As long as she could remember she had worked the fields for Mr. Hoops or helped him in the training of her puppies. And the harder she had worked, the happier she had been.

Now, all that was over. No one needed her, not even Snippet. She had nothing to do. And the days stumbled over each other endlessly.

Meanwhile, things began to go wrong at the City Hall. It wasn't anything big or important that happened. Just little things that added up to something big.

The high school band began to practice on the second floor of the City Hall, and every time the tuba hit a certain note Reddy and Snippet howled uncontrollably. It put the Mayor and Bessie, and even the four Commissioners, on edge.

Then Victoria had kittens in the coal room, and if either dog so much as passed her door, she leaped out like a tigress and clawed at them until the yelping was dreadful to hear.

On top of all this Reddy hunted in her dreams. Sometimes she found pheasant and partridge and quail. Then she would bark with joy. More often, however, she failed to jump over a fence, and moaned in a way that was half-human.

But the final incident that brought in a score of complaints was when Snippet got his nose caught in a mousetrap. He let out such a bloodcurdling cry that a woman customer at Mr. Hoops' window fell to the floor in a faint.

"Adam," said the mayor as kindly as he could, "the time has come to find a kennel for your dogs." Then at an imploring look from Katy he added, "Of course, you can wait for slightly warmer days."

# WORK TO DO

Mr. Hoops was a man who never went to *meet* trouble. He waited for it to catch up with him and tap him on the shoulder. Sometimes he even waited until it whirled him about sharply.

"Time enough," he said to Reddy and Snippet one Saturday night soon after the mousetrap incident, "time enough to think about leaving here when warm weather comes. We got through yesterday, didn't we? All right, we'll get through tomorrow too. You'll see."

And he tried to whistle a gay tune as he stirred a pot of mulligan. But every now and then the whistling stopped and was a long time starting up again.

During one of these pauses, Officer O'Toole rattled the front door. Mr. Hoops let him in and invited him downstairs to sit awhile.

"Don't offer me any of that mulligatawny, Adam. I could clean the whole pot, and what would the dogs think if I did the like of that? It smells elegant!" he sniffed.

Mr. Hoops laughed. "Occasionally I sample it myself, but I always feel like a dog when I do."

Reddy and Snippet rubbed against the officer's legs.

"It was the Mayor sent me," Officer O'Toole said, as he bent over to pat the dogs. "He stops me as he drives by and says, 'O'Toole, would you be so kind as to drop in on Adam and tell him to be sure the safe is locked? I put some mighty important papers in it, O'Toole,' he says, 'and I can't remember for the life of me whether I locked it or not. 'Twould worry me all Sunday,' he says.

"Then I gives him the green light and away he goes," chuckled the policeman. "And now I've got to skedaddle too."

Mr. Hoops saw Officer O'Toole to the door. Then he tried the handle of the safe which he had locked when the five-o'clock whistle blew. This was a firm habit with Mr. Hoops. He felt more responsibility for the city's money and papers than if they had been his own. Only the City Treasurer and the Mayor knew the combination of this safe.

With a little sigh of relief at the peace and quiet, he began to jot down all of the things he wanted to do on Monday. At the very bottom of the list he wrote hurriedly, "Look up a good kennel man." He penciled this last quite faintly, almost as if he thought that the words and the need for them might vanish over the week end.

When, the same evening, Mrs. Hoops saw Mr. Hoops come home without his hat, she knew that he was worried over something. Quite rightly, she suspected it concerned Reddy and Snippet.

And then Mrs. Hoops said something which gave Mr.

Hoops a jolt. "Just because *Reddy's* hunting days are over," she remarked, "just because of that is no reason Snippet should be neglected. Don't you think you should be hardening him so he'll be in condition for the hunting season?"

Mr. Hoops looked at Mrs. Hoops in wonderment. Every now and again she would come out with a suggestion that showed she understood dogs too.

So it was that on the following day, which was Sunday, Mr. Hoops took Snippet out alone. Before they set off together he stooped down and had a word with Reddy. Then with his eyes carefully avoiding hers, he smoothed her head and said good-by.

Reddy made no move to follow. Yet she seemed to believe they could not really go off without her, for she stood up now, waiting to be invited.

As Snippet bounded up the stairs after Mr. Hoops, Reddy scarcely breathed. She heard the sound of their footfalls along the corridor. She heard the door to the street close with a terrible finality. She ran over to the window to hear her name, no matter how softly it might be called. But no voice came. Mr. Hoops' footsteps were growing fainter and fainter now, and the click of Snippet's toenails on the sidewalk could no longer be heard at all. She gave one loud bark as a reminder to them, but the only answer was her own echo. So she stood there for a long time nosing the air coming in through the window. She could smell spring, and a great longing filled her.

With Snippet gone, the basement suddenly seemed hushed and chill. The ticking of the clock on the wall upstairs only emphasized the quiet.

Reddy walked slowly to her rug, but she was restless and could not sleep. Trembling a little, she got up and made her way to the coal room. Even a scuffle with Victoria and her kittens was to be preferred to all this stillness. But a sniff around the coal room revealed that Victoria and her entire family had gone out too. Miserably, Reddy returned to her own quarters.

Minute after minute ticked by. Finally, with a sigh of weariness, she flopped down on her rug. She had almost fallen asleep when suddenly she twitched and was wide awake. The door upstairs was opening. Then it clicked shut, quietly and quickly. A stranger was walking overhead with hurried steps.

Reddy was alert at once. She crept cautiously up the stairs, her hackles rising. Unmindful of any danger to herself she went into Mr. Hoops' office. A man stood close to the safe, his back toward Reddy. Quietly she circled him, her nose reaching out to sift his scent from the familiar belongings of Mr. Hoops.

Instinctively she disliked him and let out a low warning growl. The man wheeled about, reaching for his gun. Then with frightening quickness he began beating at Reddy with the butt end of it. The hard steel hit her, now on the shoulders, now on the flanks. Yet the shock of the blows did not confuse her thinking. It whipped her into a fury of strength. She hurled herself at the prowler with such force that he was thrown against the wall.

And to a crash of glass and brass and bells that frightened Reddy more than the blows of the gun, the wall clock came bumping down on the thief's head. With a heavy thud, he fell to the floor.

The clock was in ruins. Coiled springs, wheels, pinions, and the big shiny pendulum were spilled over the thief's chest, and the hour hand was stuck through his hair. It gave him a rakish look.

Reddy stood there puzzled. She was covered with fine splinters of glass, but none had penetrated her coat. She shook herself, stepped carefully over the glass and wire, and made her way to the man. He lay very still.

She stood guard over him. Her shoulders ached from the blows, but she did not mind the pain at all. At last she had work to do. She must hold this stranger until her master returned. Steady. Steady. He would come.

How still everything seemed! Even the ticking noise had stopped. Outside, a Sunday quiet hung over the street. Only a few sparrows were making twittering remarks to each other. The prowler groaned, but made no move.

Finally the streets began to liven with men and women and children coming home from church. But Reddy never wavered. Even when the lock turned, she stood rigid, though she knew in a flash that it was Mr. Hoops and Snippet.

Anxious to see how Reddy fared, Mr. Hoops walked hurriedly down the corridor. He gave only a passing glance into his office, but that was enough to show him the opened safe, and the thief with Reddy on guard.

At that very instant, the thief opened his eyes, but when he saw *two* red dogs where before he had seen only one, he closed them quickly again.

"Steady, Partner! Steady!" breathed Mr. Hoops. He reached for the telephone and called Officer O'Toole and the Mayor. Officer O'Toole came running, his dinner napkin

still stuffed between his brass buttons. Close on his heels followed the Mayor and two of the four Commissioners.

There was such a hubbub in the crowded cage that Mr. Hoops and his dogs slipped downstairs unnoticed.

Reddy gave one glad cry when she and Snippet and Mr. Hoops were back together again. She began to leap and run in circles around Mr. Hoops, and there was an air of importance in the very way she wagged her tail. It

reminded him of the way she used to act after a good day of hunting when things had gone just right.

Upstairs, Mayor Twitterton was saying to Policeman O'Toole, "I'm sorry I asked Adam to move his dogs out. Reddy has done the citizens of Belleville a great service today. I had no idea that the City Hall needed a watchdog. So long as I am Mayor, she and her pup shall live right here in City Hall."

And since he had already been Mayor for a dozen years, and since his campaign for Congress was not going along too well, it looked as if he would go right on being Mayor for another dozen years.

With the thief handcuffed and the two Commissioners on watch, the Mayor and Policeman O'Toole went downstairs to break the good news to Mr. Hoops.

But they got only as far as the landing. There they stopped suddenly, realizing that he must have overheard the Mayor's announcement.

"Did you hear that? Everything's going to be all right," Mr. Hoops was telling Reddy. "Snippet can take over the field work, and you have a new job guarding City Hall." Then a look of triumph crossed his face. "Why, you've got about the most important job in all Belleville!"

Too happy to say more, he swooped the great gangling dog into his arms and danced a funny little jig, in and out among Katy's mops and pails.